For all who follow the rainbow

and with special thanks

to the Hudson family

—J.N.

Over the Rainbow
Lyrics by E. Y. Harburg, Music by Harold Arlen
Copyright © 1938, 1939 Renewed 1966, 1967 Metro-Goldwyn-Mayer Inc.
Rights Assigned by EMI Catalogue Partnership
All Rights Controlled and Administered by EMI Feist Catalogue Inc.
All Rights Reserved/International Copyright Secured/Used by Permission
Illustrations copyright © 2001 by Julia Noonan
Printed in the U.S.A. All rights reserved. www.harperchildrens.com

Library of Congress Cataloging-in-Publication Data
Harburg, E. Y. (Edgar Yipsel), 1898–1981.
    Over the rainbow / by E. Y. Harburg and Harold Arlen ; illustrations by Julia Noonan. — 1st ed.
        p.   cm.
    Summary: An illustrated version of the classic song from the movie "The Wizard of Oz."
    ISBN 0-06-028949-X — ISBN 0-06-02500-7 (lib. bdg.)
    1. Children's songs—United States—Texts.   [1. Songs.]   I. Arlen, Harold, 1905–1986.   II. Noonan,
Julia, ill.   III. Title.
PZ8.3.H1969 Ov   2002   2001039680
782.42164'0268—dc21   CIP
[E]   AC

Typography by Matt Adamec   1 2 3 4 5 6 7 8 9 10   ❖   First edition

Over the Rainbow

by E. Y. Harburg and Harold Arlen
illustrations by Julia Noonan

HarperCollinsPublishers

When all the world is a hopeless jumble
and the raindrops tumble all around,

heaven opens a magic lane.

When all the clouds darken up the skyway,
there's a rainbow highway to be found,
leading from your windowpane

to a place behind the sun,
just a step beyond the rain.

Somewhere over the rainbow
way up high,
there's a land that I heard of
once in a lullaby.

Somewhere over the rainbow skies are blue,

and the dreams that you dare to dream
really do come true.

Someday I'll wish upon a star

and wake up where the clouds are far behind me,

where troubles melt like lemon drops,
away, above the chimney tops

that's where you'll find me.

Somewhere over the rainbow

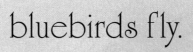

bluebirds fly.

Birds fly over the rainbow,
why then, oh why can't I?

If happy little bluebirds fly
beyond the rainbow,

why oh why can't I?

Over the Rainbow

Lyric by E. Y. Harburg • Music by Harold Arlen

Moderately (not fast)

When all the world is a hope-less jum-ble and the rain - drops tum-ble all a - round,

heav - en o-pens a mag - ic lane.

When all the clouds dark-en up the sky-way, there's a rain - bow high-way to be found,

lead - ing from your win - dow - pane to a place be-hind the

sun, just a step be-yond the rain. _____

Chorus:

Some - where o - ver the rain - bow way up high,

there's a land that I heard of once in a lull - a - by.